This book is dedicated to my incredible son.

He was diagnosed with Duchenne Muscular Dystrophy (DMD) when he was almost 4 years old.

My Son is the definition of a true warrior who will NEVER give up on the battle that lays before him!

Your mommy, sister and I are right there fighting with you now and forever!

Love,
Your Daddy
~Luke Dalien

Written by Luke Dalien

Illustrated by Linnae Dalien

Like most muskrats his age, Mark loved to play.

Climbing trees, running in the forest

and jumping around all day.

It wasn't until he was maybe 4 or 5 years old
Mark noticed his legs would often ache
and had trouble being controlled.

One day he asked his mommy
what caused his legs to feel so tired.

She wasn't exactly sure, so she brought Mark
to the doctor the family admired.

Mark and his mommy walked into the
waiting room filled with boys his own age.
He couldn't help but notice all of the boys had
legs that hurt each in a different stage.

Some walked around just like him, and some
had metal tied to the outside of their leg.

Some of the boys sat in chairs with wheels
like his new friend Matthew Greg.

Mark didn't say anything not sure what to expect.

He just sat down in a black office chair

waiting to be checked.

Finally, Mark stood up as the
doctor called his name.

As he got closer to the office with his mommy,

the more nervous he became.

After speaking with the
doctor, his mommy turned To Mark.
"They are running some tests and we will
come back soon, but now, let's go to the park."

A few weeks past and nothing seemed to change.
Mark's legs would still get tired faster than his
friends which seemed to him, strange.

Then one day, Mark's mommy received a call,
and the results were finally in.

They went back to the same doctor's office
where they had already been.

The doctor explained to Mark and his
mommy what was causing his legs to ache.
In simple terms, Mark's pain was from the
lack of a protein his body did not make.

He explained that everyone's bodies are
different and sometimes things go wrong.
For Mark it was nothing he did at all, his
muscles just weren't as strong.

The doctor let both Mark and his mommy

know how everything will progress.

"The important thing to remember," he said,

"is to make sure you get plenty of rest."

"If your muscles feel sore, sit down for awhile until you feel better."

He handed Mark's mommy a bunch of
material including a long letter.

They set up another appointment and were told to write their questions on a list. Doctors around the world are working hard to find a cure, though one doesn't currently exist.

As they left the office, Mark could see there
was sadness on his mommy's face.
"It's okay mommy," he said, "there's plenty
of time left in this race."

Perhaps it's true Mark didn't fully
understand the situation he was in.
Or maybe he was born a true fighter who
only knew one thing, to win.

The road of life can be rocky and
unpaved in certain spots.
There's just no time to sit around and
fill your mind with negative thoughts.

The greatest chance that Mark has in life
along with others who have the same disease
is to raise your voice, break out your fists and
help bring Muscular Dystrophy to its knees!

THE END

Author Luke Dalien has spent his life dedicated to helping others break the chains of normal so that they may live fulfilled lives. When he's not busy creating books aimed to bring a smile to the faces of children, he and his amazing wife, Suzie, work tirelessly on their joint passion; helping children with special needs reach their excellence. Together, they founded an online tutoring and resource company, **SpecialEdResource.com.**

Poetry, which had been a personal endeavor of Luke's for the better part of 2 decades, was mainly reserved for his beautiful wife, and their 2 amazing children, Lily and Alex. With several "subtle nudges" from his family, Luke finally decided to share his true passion in creativity with the world through his first children's book series, "The Adventures Of The Silly Little Beaver".

With a recent development, Luke decided to start this second series, "Mark the Mighty Muskrat" dealing with the personal struggles his family is going through after one of their children was diagnosed with Duchenne Muscular Dystrophy.

Illustrator Linnae Dalien grew up in Minnesota where she raised 2 adoring children with her husband, Larry. Always creative, she found her passion in designing and editing photographs until they achieve that "perfect look." It wasn't long before family and friends began reaching out requesting her to work on their own photographs for a variety of special occasions.

It was during that part of her life that her creativity took a turn and a new passion was born. Linnae discovered her true artistic ability as she began doodling and drawing different characters to aide in some of the photographs she was working on. Reaching out to her son, Luke, regarding her new found love for drawing, they decided to join forces and launched their first book series, "The Adventures Of The Silly Little Beaver".

Linnae is again joining forces with Author Luke Dalien to create this new series, "Mark the Might Muskrat".

For a full animated version of this book along with others written by Luke Dalien, please visit our website; www.LilexStudios.com

The Adventures of theSilly Little Beaver

Released October 2018

Coming Soon

Coming Soon

Coming Soon

Many other books in this series will be released soon.

For a full animated versions of these books along with others written by Luke Dalien, please visit our website; www.LilexStudios.com

Made in the USA
Coppell, TX
08 February 2021